You Can Swim, Jim

You can Swim, Jim

Kaye Umansky &
Margaret Chamberlain

THE BODLEY HEAD · LONDON

SPLASH! Whoopee! Hey, look at me!
I'm first one in, the water's fine!

Sam don't howl. You've lost your towel?
Never mind, I'll lend you mine.

Jilly says she's feeling chilly.

Clive can dive. Look! There he goes!

Come on in, Jim. You can swim, Jim.
Take a jump and hold your nose.

Look at Jeannie's
wee bikini.
That looks lovely.
Is it new?

Sore eyes, Doreen?
That's the chlorine.
Goggles
are the thing for you.

Clark has got a rubber shark
(A birthday present from his gran).

Don't look grim, Jim. You can swim, Jim.
You can swim, you know you can.

Kate does handstands underwater.
Wow! That's great, Kate, we're impressed!

Lola's lying on her lilo,
Says she needs a little rest.

Gail's pretending she's a whale.
Watch her do a water-spout!

Come on in, Jim. You can swim, Jim.
Come on in, don't hang about.

Walt is swimming underwater.
Says he is a submarine.

What d'you say, Fay? Hip hooray!
They're turning on the wave machine!

This is what I call a giggle!
Hold on tight now, everyone.

Will you come, Jim. Don't look glum, Jim.
Come on in, it's so much fun.

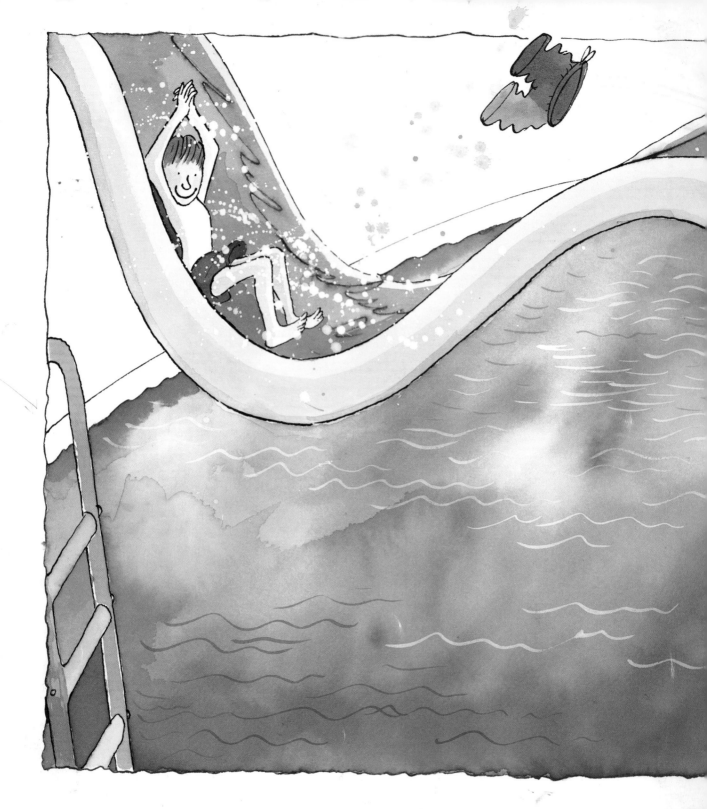

Brad's gone mad! He's up the ladder!
Now he's sliding down the chute!

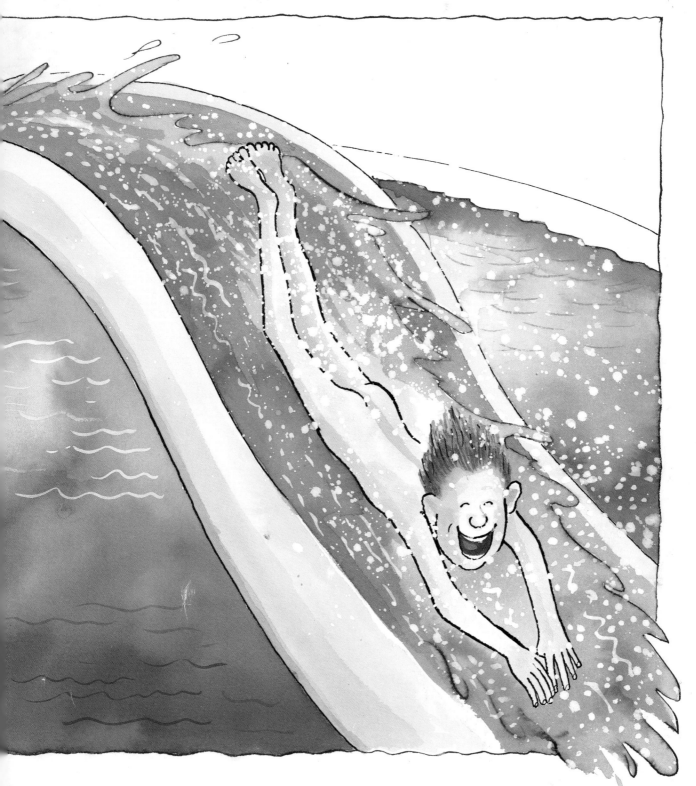

That was speedy, yes indeedy.
(Shame about his bathing suit.)

Jim looks grumpy, gone all humpy.
Says he doesn't want a dip.

Going off to buy some biscuits –
Mind, it's slippy! Jim don't trip!

SPLASH! He's fallen in the water!
What a great catastrophe!

Jim's in trouble! Lots of bubbles!
Where's he gone? Oh deary me!

Up he bobs and look, he's smiling!
Hey there, you lot, watch him go!

You can swim, Jim! You can swim, Jim!
You can swim! I told you so!

3 5 7 9 10 8 6 4 2
Copyright © text Kaye Umansky 1997
Copyright © illustrations Margaret Chamberlain 1997
Designed by Rowan Seymour

Kaye Umansky and Margaret Chamberlain have asserted their rights
under the Copyright, Designs and Patents Act, 1988
to be identified as the author and illustrator of this work

First published in the United Kingdom 1997
by The Bodley Head Children's Books
Random House, 20 Vauxhall Bridge Road, London SW1V 2SA

Random House Australia (Pty) Limited
20 Alfred Street, Milsons Point, Sydney,
New South Wales 2061, Australia

Random House New Zealand Limited
18 Poland Road, Glenfield,
Auckland 10, New Zealand

Random House South Africa (Pty) Limited
PO Box 2263, Rosebank 2121, South Africa

Random House UK Limited Reg. No. 954009

A CIP catalogue record for this book is available
from the British Library

ISBN 0 370 324528

Printed in Hong Kong